Halloween with
Snowman Paul

Written by Yossi Lapid
Illustrated by Joanna Pasek

ISBN 978-0-9973899-1-3

In loving memory of Sanyi

Strange aliens will spot you.

They'll come at a fast pace.

They'll lift you to their spaceship.

You'll vanish in deep space!

Warning #2

No entry!

Don't dare go past this doorpost.
It's the forbidden path!
But if you do,
we're warning you:
You'll taste the witch's wrath!

She'll put you on her broomstick,

And fly you to her house.

She'll feed you a green potion.

You'll turn into a mouse!

Don't dare climb up this ladder.
Your next step will be too much.
But if you do, we're warning you:
You'll feel a scary touch!

A dragon will approach you,
And take you on a ride.

He'll bring you to a party,
Where dragons dance outside!

He'll sneak up close behind you,
And scare you with a "BOO!"

You'll try hard to escape him.

He'll chase right after you!

Oh wow, you're here already!
We're happy that you came.

It's Halloween, so step right in.
Let's play a spooky game!

We'll sit around this table,
And sing a scary song.

Let's huddle all together,
In case something goes wrong!

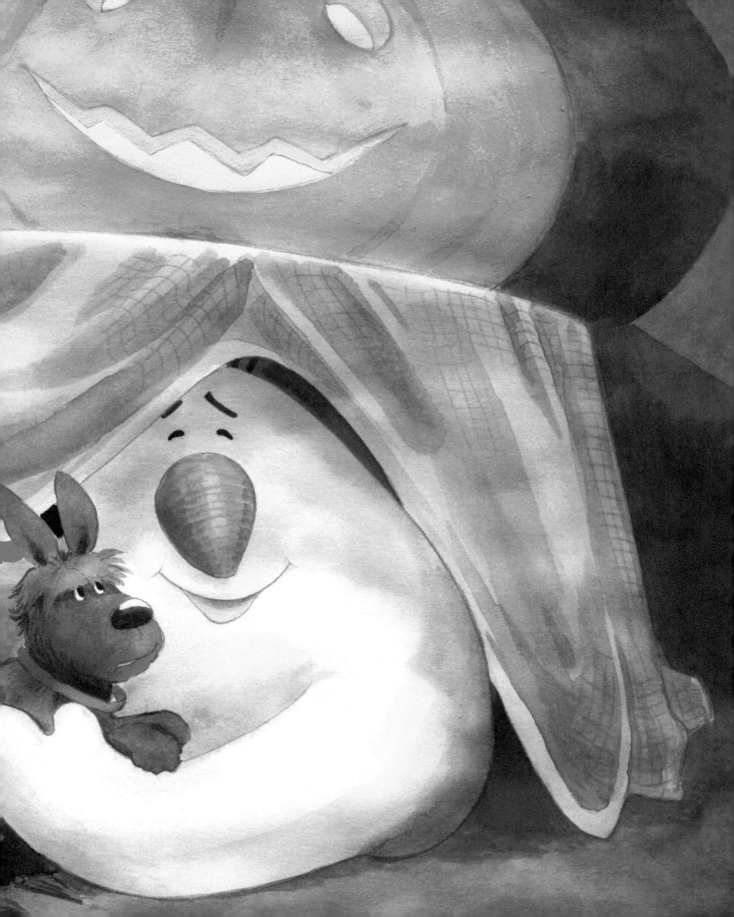

Hey, don't you leave this tree house.
Our game is not quite through.

But if you do, we've put aside
Some yummy treats for you!